To every thing
there is a Season

Aldred

To Every Thing There Is a Season

Verses from Ecclesiastes

ILLUSTRATIONS BY

LEO & DIANE DILLON

THE BLUE SKY PRESS

An Imprint of Scholastic Inc.

To BONNIE VERBURG, who has given our thoughts form with Ecclesiastes;

to KATHY WESTRAY, for caring about the details;

and to our son, LEE DILLON, who has been a source of inspiration.

THE BLUE SKY PRESS

Illustrations copyright © 1998 by Leo & Diane Dillon

The text in this book is from the King James Version of the Bible, Chapter III, verses 1–8, followed by Chapter I, verse 4. The language has been slightly adapted for young readers.

We gratefully acknowledge the invaluable assistance provided by
Peter J. Gomes, Plummer Professor of Christian Morals and Pusey Minister in The Memorial Church,
Harvard University; Dr. Lawrence Schiffman, Professor of Hebrew and Judaic Studies, New York University; and
William L. Fash, Bowditch Professor of Central American and Mexican Archaeology and Ethnology, Harvard University,
for their expertise in the research for this book.

Library of Congress catalog card number: 97-35124

10 9 8 7 6 5 4   9/9 0/0 01 02 03

ISBN 0-590-47887-7

Special thanks to Richard Robinson for his vision and support.

Production supervision by Angela Biola   Designed by Leo & Diane Dillon and Kathleen Westray
Printed in Mexico   49
First printing, October 7, 1998

About Ecclesiastes

THE TIMELESS PASSAGES in this book have been a source of inspiration, hope, and comfort for millions of people around the world. They were written more than two thousand years ago, yet they encompass the full range of contemporary human emotion and experience, from the wonders of birth to the unanswered questions of death. Scores of generations have quoted these verses at weddings, funerals, graduations, birth celebrations, and religious ceremonies; they have also been popularized in songs, books, theatre, and motion pictures.

The text in this book is taken from the King James Version of the Bible, the Book of Ecclesiastes, Chapter III, verses 1–8, followed by Chapter I, verse 4. The Book of Ecclesiastes is one of the five *megilloth* in the third part of the Jewish Tanakh. Although it is commonly attributed to Solomon, the actual authorship is unknown; research indicates that it dates back to the third or fourth century B.C.

The poet Tennyson called Ecclesiastes "the greatest poem of ancient or modern times." *To Every Thing There Is a Season* presents these famous words as a celebration of the seasons of human existence — the mysterious ebb and flow of happiness and pain that is ultimately beyond our control. Yet no matter what our experience, we always return to the idea that there is a time and a purpose to our lives and to the world around us.

TO EVERY THING THERE IS A SEASON,
AND A TIME TO EVERY PURPOSE UNDER THE HEAVEN:

A TIME TO BE BORN,

AND A TIME TO DIE;

A TIME TO PLANT,

AND A TIME TO PLUCK UP THAT WHICH IS PLANTED;

A TIME TO KILL,

AND A TIME TO HEAL;

A TIME TO BREAK DOWN,

AND A TIME TO BUILD UP;

A TIME TO WEEP,

AND A TIME TO LAUGH;

A TIME TO MOURN,

AND A TIME TO DANCE;

A TIME TO CAST AWAY STONES,

AND A TIME TO GATHER STONES TOGETHER;

A TIME TO EMBRACE,

AND A TIME TO REFRAIN FROM EMBRACING;

A TIME TO GET,

AND A TIME TO LOSE;

A TIME TO KEEP,

AND A TIME TO CAST AWAY;

A TIME TO REND,

AND A TIME TO SEW;

A TIME TO KEEP SILENCE,

AND A TIME TO SPEAK;

A TIME TO LOVE,

AND A TIME TO HATE;

A TIME OF WAR,

AND A TIME OF PEACE.

ONE GENERATION PASSES AWAY, AND ANOTHER GENERATION COMES: BUT THE EARTH ABIDES FOR EVER.

For more information about the illustrations in this book, please turn the page.

About the Illustrations

The timeless words from Ecclesiastes remind us that there are things in life that all people share, regardless of our diverse beliefs and cultures. Our way of illustrating this was to present unique styles of art from around the world, each one depicting a single phrase of text.

From pre-historic times through the present, the need to express the human spirit artistically has persisted. Much of what we know about ancient cultures is gathered through the study of architecture, sculpture, painting, and artifacts. We have been inspired by art in its many forms and, with this book, respectfully pay homage to it, and to those things all people have in common.

The graphic source for each illustration and the media we have used are described below. The dates signify the approximate period of the art style that inspired us.

To every thing there is a season, and a time to every purpose under the heaven:

Ireland — Early illuminated manuscript style from the seventh and eighth centuries A.D. One of the best-known examples of this art is the *Book of Kells*, a richly decorated Latin text of the four Gospels.

Gouache on brown parchment paper

A time to be born, and a time to die;

Egypt — Created in the style of murals painted on the walls of tombs during the New Kingdom, roughly between 2000 – 1000 B.C. Anubis, the god of mummification, assists the deceased to the underworld. Life is given and, ultimately, taken away.

Acrylic paint on three-ply Bristol board

a time to plant, and a time to pluck up that which is planted;

Japan — The ukiyo-e (the floating world) woodblock prints depicted secular life and pleasures, reaching their height in the eighteenth and nineteenth centuries A.D. Workers plant their crops early on so there will be food to harvest at the end of the season.

Ink and watercolor on paper

A time to kill, and a time to heal;

Mexico — Pre-conquest, Mixtec, screen-fold picture books were read forward and backward and date back to the seventh century A.D. A well-known example is the Codex Nuttal, a picture manuscript from ancient Mexico. Giving one's life for one's beliefs is considered an honor. Sacrifice is also offered as proof of gratitude and devotion.

Acrylic paint on three-ply Bristol board

a time to break down, and a time to build up;

    Greece — Red-and-black figure, classical vase painting dates back to the sixth century B.C. Scenes of daily life, sports, theatre, education, and the realm of the gods were depicted on vessels for everyday use as well as for use in ceremonies. In times of war, soldiers demolish buildings and monuments; in peaceful times, people build them up.

    Ink and acrylic paint on scratchboard

A time to weep, and a time to laugh;

    India — Illustrations for manuscripts reached their zenith during the Mughal Dynasty in the early sixteenth and seventeenth centuries A.D. Drought and famine often lead to starvation and separation, while times of plenty allow for a joyful life and happy reunions.

    Acrylic paint on three-ply Bristol board

a time to mourn, and a time to dance;

    Europe — In the Middle Ages, with the invention of the printing press, books were illustrated with woodcut art ranging from intricate decoration to pictorial statement. This style with shadow lines is from fifteenth-century Germany A.D. The passing of a loved one brings grief, while the union of a couple in matrimony is a time for festive dancing.

    Ink and watercolor on Bristol board

A time to cast away stones, and a time to gather stones together;

    North America — Mural painting style from a kiva (ceremonial space) in the Kuaua Pueblo of the fourteenth century A.D. The Anasazi people built stone structures up to five stories high. Stones are removed from the fields to allow plants to grow, and then they are used for construction.

    Gouache on three-ply Bristol board

a time to embrace, and a time to refrain from embracing;

    Ethiopia — In the late seventeenth to early eighteenth century A.D., Lake Tana and Gonder formed an important center where books were illustrated and copied for Gonderine kings. People embrace in a spirit of friendship and refrain from embracing while conducting the practical matters of business.

    Gouache on three-ply Bristol board

A time to get, and a time to lose;

    Thailand (formerly Siam) — Intricate figures were lit from behind and projected onto a screen for a shadow play, an art form that has existed for centuries. Families acquire possessions, but they also lose them.

    Ink and acrylic paint on acetate

a time to keep, and a time to cast away;

China — Silk manufacturing techniques were developed between 2000 – 1000 B.C. For centuries, paintings were done on silk in addition to paper, using ink and watercolor. Large fish are kept and eaten, but the small fish are returned to the water to grow.

Gouache painted on silk, mounted on paper

A time to rend, and a time to sew;

Russia — Icon paintings were done not only for the church and monastery, but they hung in almost every home. The high point of this art was from the twelfth to the sixteenth century A.D. Fabrics are divided and torn in order to sew together new garments.

Acrylic paint on three-ply Bristol board

a time to keep silence, and a time to speak;

Australia — Traditional aboriginal bark painting is called the x-ray style because it shows the internal organs and spinal columns of animals and fish. Observers keep silent while watching wildlife; later, stories are told about the animals seen. Date unknown.

Gouache on bark paper

A time to love, and a time to hate;

The Far North (from Siberia to Greenland) — Stone-cut art by the Inuit people is a form of printmaking developed in the nineteenth century A.D. Parents feel intense love for their children and despise any evil that threatens them.

Ink and acrylic paint on scratchboard

a time of war, and a time of peace.

Middle East — Iranian miniatures were meant for intimate viewing to appreciate their intricate detail. The artists from the Herat school were highly prized during the Safavid Dynasty in the early sixteenth century A.D. Clashes between people sometimes lead to war and bloodshed, but harmony and understanding lead to peace and happiness.

Acrylic and gilt painted on acetate

One generation passes away, and another generation comes: but the earth abides for ever.

Earth, as seen from outer space. The blue planet called home.

Pastel frisket and ink on three-ply Bristol board